P9-BXZ-771

THE ADVENTURES OF PELICAN PETE

FIRST DISCOVERIES

For Trevor & Gavin

May your
curiosity
lead you to
fantastic
firsts and
delightful
discoveries

St. Augustine
1/4/17

FRANCES KEISER

ILLUSTRATED BY HUGH KEISER

Explore!

Frances R Keiser

Sagaponack Books • Saint Augustine

We wish to acknowledge the following experts for their accuracy checks:

William R. Adams, Ph.D., Director, Department of Heritage Tourism, City of St. Augustine
John H. Hann, Site Historian at Mission San Luis
Karen Harvey, Writer, Historian
Jerald Milanich, Curator in Archaeology, Florida Museum of Natural History
David Nolan, Author, *The Houses of St. Augustine*
James A. Rodgers Jr., Biological Scientist IV, Wildlife Research Laboratory, FFWCC
Rosanne Sanchez (Isleta Pueblo), All Indian Pueblo Council, Inc., Albuquerque, NM
Wayne Wheeler, President, United States Lighthouse Society

Thanks to:

Family, friends, and colleagues who freely give their support, advice, and expertise; children, parents, grandparents, and teachers who enthusiastically give their opinions and encouragement; the residents of St. Augustine and surrounding areas for loving and pre- serving our city, and especially to: Jim Collis, Michael Cunningham, Tara and Matt Dunn, Tim Fast, Teresa Garris, Kerry and David Hadas, Karen Harvey, Beth Mansbridge, Dena and Steve Meyerhoff, Oscar Sosa, James Rodgers, and Jim Runyeon.

Keiser, Frances.
    First discoveries / by Frances Keiser; Illustrated by Hugh Keiser — 32 p., 26 cm.
  (The adventures of Pelican Pete ; 3)
    SUMMARY: Pete visits Saint Augustine, Florida, our nation's oldest city and discovers its rich history, our responsibility to the land, and the need for habitat preservation.
  Audience: Ages 4-8.
  LCCN: 2001118422
  ISBN 13: 978-0-9668845-2-4
  ISBN 10: 0-9668845-2-3
  1. Pelicans—Juvenile fiction. 2. Ecology—Juvenile fiction. 3. Saint Augustine (Fla.)—History—Juvenile fiction. [1. Pelicans—Fiction. 2. Ecology—Fiction. 3. Saint Augustine (Fla.)—History—Fiction.] 4. Stories in rhyme. I. Keiser, Hugh, ill. II. Title: First discoveries. III. Title: Pelican Pete.

PZ8.3.K273Fi 2002   [E]

10 9 8 7 6 5 4 3
Text Copyright © 2002 by Frances Keiser
Illustrations Copyright © 2002 by Hugh Keiser
All rights reserved. No part of this book may be reproduced in any manner without permission in writing from the publisher, except in the case of brief excerpts in critical reviews and articles. Inquiries should be made by calling 800-450-7383 or addressed to Sagaponack Books, 7324 A1A South, St. Augustine, FL 32080
www.SagaponackBooks.com

Printed and bound in Canada by Friesens
Third Printing 2007

For all those individuals who are working to preserve and restore habitat for wildlife at their homes, schools, workplaces, and communities.

"Will you teach your children what we have taught our children? . . . What befalls the earth befalls the children of the earth. This we know: the earth does not belong to man, man belongs to the earth. . . . Man did not weave the web of life, he is merely a strand in it. Whatever he does to the web, he does to himself."

—Seathl, Squamish (Chief Seattle)

The Pelican Pete series

A Bird Is Born
Preening for Flight
First Discoveries
Annie the River Otter
Un Ave Nace (A Bird Is Born - Spanish)

Member of the Green Press Initiative
Printed on Recycled Paper

For all the children good and sweet:
I'll tell a tale of Pelican Pete;
And for all who are curious today,
I'll tell the story just this way:

Pete's a bird who's fun to know,
Having adventures high and low.
So let's join Pete and follow his trail
From high in the air, where we start our tale ...

While soaring over the blue-green sea,
Cruising the waves and happy to be
Playing with his feathered friends,
Ignoring the time when daylight ends,

Pete notices a light circling around
In a regular beat high off the ground.
It flashes his eyes, then shines to sea;
Curious, Pete wonders, "What can that be?"

So, very early the following day,
As the sun rises a dawning ray,
Pete flies to the north until he sees
A tall white tower jutting through the trees—

Spiraled in black like candy canes,
Crowned in red with windowpanes
Through which a rotating prism lens
Sends beams of light through curves and bends,

Warning ships near and far
Of approaching coast and high sandbar.
Pete lands on top, silent as a hawk,
Above the circular gallery walk,

To view the surrounding scenery:
Inlets, bays, rivers, and sea.
And far in the distance a shimmering sight
Like ruby jewels in the morning light:

Rising above trees of green,
The red tile roofs of St. Augustine.
But in order to visit this wonderful place,
A Bridge of Lions you must face.

"A Bridge of Lions! How can that be?
This is something I *must* go and see!
Roaring lions spanning a river?
Just the thought makes me quiver!"

As he approaches the city's splendor,
A bridge he sees, with draw and tender.
And standing guard, each on a pedestal throne,
Are two ENORMOUS lions ... made completely of stone.

Pete sighs in relief as he understands,
Our imagination sometimes expands
To create fantasies that make us feel
Scared or happy, but they're not always real.

Looking about, Pete likes what he sees:
Beautiful buildings with balconies,
Fountains, statues, and colorful flowers;
Plazas, churches, and ringing bell towers.

And behind them all, atop a hill,
A mighty fort where soldiers drill.
Wearing coats and caps of another time,
Iron cannons they fire and prime.

Flying low over cobblestone streets,
Pete hears how the Spanish sailed in fleets.
Leaving Spain for treasure's lure,
Discovering lands they'd not seen before,

To claim them for the Spanish throne:
Another realm to rule and own.
But when they arrived, they were not alone,
Natives called this land their home.

People lived here thousands of years,
Hunting game with arrows and spears,
Planting crops, gathering food,
Living among a multitude

Of plants and creatures of every kind;
Man and nature were intertwined.
The people learned to respect and treasure
Earthly gifts of every measure.

Mammals, insects, birds, and fish,
And woodland plants for every dish;
They offered seeds, berries, and fruit,
Nuts, vegetables, and tubers to root.

When the Europeans came to stay,
The natives taught them nature's way.
Stewards of the land we learned to be,
Our valued trust through history.

But all those lessons seem forgotten or lost,
And now we are paying a heavy cost.
Wild environments have been displaced;
Man's developments have taken their place.

Native flowers and trees are uprooted
For lawns and shrubs that are just not suited
To provide shelter, homes, and food
For all the creatures we now exclude.

By clearing land for us to build,
Plants and animals are being killed.
But it doesn't have to be this way.
We can leave the animals some room to stay.

When building houses, schools, and workplaces,
Always preserve some natural spaces.
And in our backyards we can create
Wildlife habitats that will make

Suitable homes for fascinating creatures
Of varied shapes and unusual features.
Being close to nature helps you understand
We can all live *together* on Earth's sea and land.

Now that Pete's left the City Gate,
His adventurous nature can hardly wait.
Curious birds need to travel and roam,
To fly beyond their familiar home.

Visiting new towns, habitats, and places;
Making new friends, seeing new faces.
There's so much to learn, discover, and see.
With a wing, Pete beckons, "Come along with me!"

Did You Know?

- Pelicans are social birds with keen eyesight and hearing. They often fly in a single line playing a "follow the leader" type of game. They ride thermal currents high into the air, glide, soar and fly into the valleys between the ocean waves, their wings almost touching the water. Sometimes they do this to conserve energy—but other times, pelicans seem to do it just for fun.

- Throughout history, man has used light to signal or warn ships. Each lighthouse has a daymark, a distinctive pattern or shape easily recognizable during the day, and a nightmark characterized by the length or pattern of the flash of light seen at night.

- Many lighthouses are still in use today, including the St. Augustine Lighthouse, which has a First Order Fresnel lens with over 370 revolving prisms. Its daymark is a 165-foot tall white tower with a distinctive broad black spiral and a red top. At night, its beam flashes at 30-second intervals and can be seen from 25 nautical miles away.

- The Bridge of Lions, listed on the National Register of Historic Places, is a Mediterranean Revival style drawbridge. Its two Carrara marble lions are modeled after the pair at the Loggia dei Lanzi in Florence, Italy, and stand over ten feet tall on their pedestals.

- St. Augustine is the oldest continuously occupied settlement of European origin in the continental United States. It was colonized by an expedition of settlers from Spain led by Pedro Menéndez de Avilés under orders from Spain's King Phillip II in 1565, fifty-five years before the Pilgrims landed at Plymouth Rock and forty-two years before the English colonized Jamestown.

- St. Augustine's fort is the Castillo (Cas-tee-yo) de San Marcos, built of coquina stone and completed in 1695. The Castillo, a national monument, is the only original fort built in the 17th century that is still standing intact in the United States. It survived two major sieges and was never captured by an enemy in battle.

- Henry Flagler revitalized St. Augustine in the 1880s. His architects drew their inspiration from throughout the Mediterranean region, including Venice, North Africa, and Spain. Red tile roofs were a characteristic signature of these styles.

- Nearly all Native American cultures have a creation story explaining how they came to be. Most archaeologists believe that indigenous peoples have been in the Americas for about 15,000 years. When the Europeans arrived, the area now known as St. Augustine was the village of Seloy, named after the chief of the Timucua-speaking people living there.

- The Timucuas lived in houses thatched with palm fronds, and the men wore top-knotted hair and tattooed their bodies. They cultivated corn and other plants, and also relied on hunting, fishing, and gathering wild foods.

- Habitat is the life support system for all plants and animals. Development is one of the main causes of habitat destruction, and loss of habitat is the primary cause of the extinction of species.

- Providing wildlife habitat—food, water, cover, and places to raise young—is easy to achieve, and plants are the key. Native plants meet the food and cover needs of all the animals from that particular area and can be used to restore the ecosystem. Native plants are also easier to maintain than lawns or exotic plants, requiring less water and fertilizer.

To Learn More

About pelicans:
Discover places pelicans like to gather and see them up close; these include piers, bridges, and docks where people go regularly to fish. Visit a wildlife rehabilitation center. You can locate them by consulting the "Wildlife Rehabilitation Directory" on the Internet. You will find state agencies, wildlife refuges, and sanctuaries on the Web through FloridaConservation.org. Visit your local library or bookstore for books on pelicans.

About lighthouses:
Visit the lighthouses and maritime museums in your area. Go to your local library and bookstore for books on lighthouses. Contact organizations such as the U.S. Lighthouse Society in San Francisco, CA. Surf the Web, where good information can be found at the National Park Service's Maritime Heritage site, the U.S. Coast Guard's Lighthouses site, and other sites including those of many of our nation's lighthouses, such as StAugustineLighthouse.com.

About St. Augustine:
Tour St. Augustine: There are over 50 museums, historic sites, and cultural sites to visit. St. Augustine and its environs also have many diverse habitats and natural areas to explore. Go to your local library and bookstore for books on St. Augustine. Contact organizations such as the St. Augustine Historical Society, the St. Augustine Trust for Historic Preservation, and the St. Augustine Visitor Information Center. Surf the Web: StAugustine.com and OldCity.com are good sites, and the National Park Service's web site is a good place to learn about the Castillo de San Marcos, Fort Matanzas, and other national parks and monuments.

About Native Americans:
Locate reservations, pueblos, or other lands of Native Americans. Speak to them about their language, culture, and history. Attend cultural events and ceremonies open to the public. Visit local history and heritage museums. Go to your local library or bookstore for books on indigenous peoples. Surf the Web. Some organizations with useful sites include: the Administration for Native Americans, the National Congress of American Indians, Native Web, Indigenous Peoples Biodiversity Information Network, the Bureau of Indian Affairs, and Hanksville.org.

About wildlife habitats:
Explore wild places in your area such as forests, parks, reserves, preserves, and sanctuaries. Go to your local library and bookstore for books on creating, restoring, and preserving wildlife habitats and landscaping with native plants. The National Wildlife Federation not only gives you all the information you need to create a backyard wildlife habitat, they will also certify it. Other sources of information include your county or university agricultural cooperative extension office, city or county wildflower garden clubs, and local nurseries. Organizations with helpful web sites include: the National Wildlife Federation, the U.S. Fish and Wildlife Service, FloridaConservation.org which also has links to your own state resource agency, the Native Plant Conservation Initiative, Lady Bird Johnson Wildflower Center, (your state) Native Plant Society, Wild Ones Ltd., and KidsPlanet.org.

Photograph by Oscar Sosa

About Hugh and Frances:

Hugh Keiser, a graduate of The Cooper Union, has been painting and drawing professionally for over forty years. His exploration of computers as an art medium and discovering our clown prince of birds—the brown pelican—led Hugh to create his popular children's book illustrations. He has received numerous awards for his artwork, which can be seen in public and private collections around the world.

Frances Keiser, a master naturalist and wildlife rescue volunteer, has over thirty years' experience working in the areas of wildlife conservation and early childhood education. Her background, coupled with a lifetime of poetry writing and studies in children's literature, led Frances to craft her award-winning rhyming stories and interactive school presentations.

The Keisers live with their two cats, Katie and Sparky, on a St. Augustine Florida, barrier island where wildlife abounds, children explore, and curious pelicans fly overhead.

About the Publisher:

Sagaponack Books publishes children's picture books to support Earth's beauty, habitats, and wildlife for continuing generations. Each book encourages children to understand and appreciate the natural world, instilling a desire to protect it. Sagaponack Books donates a portion of its revenue to benefit wildlife, the environment, and education.

To learn more, visit our Web site at www.PelicanPete.com.